LOST BUT ALIVE

LOYAL PAIN

SUMEET KUMAR

Sumeet Kumar, an adult who experiences several stages of love in his life, stumbles multiple times yet never gives up and moves forward; in reality, he is both a writer and a singer (as a hobby).

An extremely exciting and interesting fact about her is that he is a writer of the new era, meaning he began his writing journey at a young age while still attending school.

His some famous works i.e. Maturity Of Love (Genre - Love),Privacy For Dream (Genre - Middle Class), Army Squad ofLove (Genre- The Seperation of Army Love), 5 Days of Love(Genre- Temporarily Love), The Endearment Of Love(Genre - Historical Era Of Love), Social Destruction Indo-Pak (Genre - The Story of The Love At The Time Of Division Of India And Pakistan), Middle Class Soul (Genre - The Dreams of Middle Class), The Accursed Kanatpur (Genre -The Horrific Story Of A Village), Wrong Number (Genre -The Suspenseful Physco Killer Story), The Secrecy OfDeadly Midnight (Genre - The Suspense About a Crime),Fragile Religious Of Death (Genre- The Death Of A TrustfulPerson), Nature Vs Science (Genre - The Future Battle Between Nature And Science In A Horrific Way), Generic Man (Genre - The Dream of I.I.T), The Unconsious 12 Hours(Genre - The Illusion At Stage Of Comma), The StrangeBurden (Genre - The Burden Of Love) , Her Existence (Genre- The Female Pain In The Society) , Jockstrap Prize (Genre -The True Story Of A National Athlete) , H Man [Hindi] (Genre - Superhero Tragic Story), H Man [English] (Genre - Superhero Tragic Story) , Maturity Of Love [Englsih] (Genre - Love) and many more are available on various geners on the offcial platform of Amazon, Flipkart and Notionpress. You can buy them from there.

Contents

Contents

Foreword

*First of all, I wholeheartedly thank all of you for choosing me.
I do not know why you chose me, but I do know this much —
my readers are not just readers; they are a part of my existence.
I am just an artist, but my real art is all of you, who have
deemed me worthy of presenting my emotions, my words, and
my thoughts before you.
My only request to you is to embrace this book with the same
love, the same connection, and the same intimacy as you have
embraced my previous works.*

— Sumit Kumar

Preface

Love is not always a mutual exchange. Sometimes it is a silent companion, a shadow that follows without acknowledgment, a truth that exists in the spaces between words and glances. This book is an exploration of that quiet, haunting love—the one that lives inside you, shaping you, teaching you, breaking you and rebuilding you in ways unseen.

I wrote this not to seek answers or to be understood, but to bear witness to the weight of one-sided love. To those who have carried it alone, who have smiled through pain, who have found beauty in the ache—this is for you. Here, silence is voice, sorrow is language, and every unsaid word finds a home.

Sumeet Kumar, an adult who experiences several stages of love in his life, stumbles multiple times yet never gives up and moves forward; in reality, he is both a writer and a singer (as a hobby).

An extremely exciting and interesting fact about her is that he is a writer of the new era, meaning he began his writing journey at a young age while still attending school.

His some famous works i.e. Maturity Of Love (Genre - Love),Privacy For Dream (Genre - Middle Class), Army Squad ofLove (Genre- The Seperation of Army Love), 5 Days of Love(Genre- Temporarily Love), The Endearment Of Love(Genre - Historical Era Of Love), Social Destruction Indo-Pak (Genre - The Story of The Love At The Time Of Division Of India And

ACKNOWLEDGEMENTS

Pakistan), Middle Class Soul (Genre - The Dreams of Middle Class), The Accursed Kanatpur (Genre -The Horrific Story Of A Village), Wrong Number (Genre -The Suspenseful Physco Killer Story), The Secrecy OfDeadly Midnight (Genre - The Suspense About a Crime),Fragile Religious Of Death (Genre- The Death Of A TrustfulPerson), Nature Vs Science (Genre - The Future Battle Between Nature And Science In A Horrific Way), Generic Man (Genre - The Dream of I.I.T), The Unconsious 12 Hours(Genre - The Illusion At Stage Of Comma), The StrangeBurden (Genre - The Burden Of Love) , Her Existence (Genre- The Female Pain In The Society) , Jockstrap Prize (Genre -The True Story Of A National Athlete) , H Man [Hindi] (Genre - Superhero Tragic Story), H Man [English] (Genre - Superhero Tragic Story) , Maturity Of Love [Englsih] (Genre - Love) and many more are available on various geners on the offcial platform of Amazon, Flipkart and Notionpress. You can buy them from there.

Prologue

I had heard long ago that one-sided love slowly hollows a person, leaving behind a silence heavier than words. But no words could prepare me for the truth of it. It seeps into the corners of your mind, lingers in your chest, and becomes a quiet companion in every breath. It is unspoken, unanswered, yet unbearably present—shaping who you are without mercy.

This book is not a story of reciprocation or triumph. It is a chronicle of living with a love that was never returned, of surviving without closure, and of discovering how much the heart can endure when it is both broken and alive.

Every memory, every pause, every tear has its own language, and through these pages, I invite you to listen.

1

BREATHE BUT DEAD

I had heard long ago that one-sided love slowly ruins a person, that it hollows them from within and leaves behind a silence heavier than words. But I never truly understood its meaning until it began to live inside me. Now I feel it in every breath I take, in every moment I try to remain calm. Its impact is so deep that even my silence has become my witness. I no longer need to speak for my pain to be known—my quietness carries the weight of everything I cannot say.

Even after crying until my eyes burn and my chest aches, I find that I cannot separate myself from this feeling. No matter how much I try to pull away, it clings to me like a shadow that follows me everywhere. This love—unreturned, unanswered—has become my only truth. It passes through my face, settles in my eyes, and reveals itself in the way I pause before speaking, in the way I look away when memories rise without permission.

Perhaps the reason I keep losing myself is also the only happiness I have ever known. There is a strange comfort in loving without being loved back, a painful beauty in holding *onto something that was never meant to stay. Every single drop of my sorrow feels alive, as if it is asking me questions about who I am, what I deserve, and how much a heart can endure before it learns to let go.*

But these questions remain unanswered. I carry them alone, heavy and unresolved, because I do not yet know how to solve them. And maybe that is what one-sided love truly does—it does not destroy you all at once. Instead, it teaches you how to survive with unanswered questions, how to smile with a broken heart, and how to live with a love that was never yours, yet became everything you were.

2

ACCEPT THE CONFUSION

Every habit of mine has been given someone else's name, as if my life were a corridor lined with borrowed identities. Yet deep within, I know the truth: I am the only reason these habits exist. No one imposed them on me; no one forced my hands or shaped my silence. My own footsteps have never lied to me—they echo with honesty, even when I try not to listen.

And yet, now, every time my eyes fall upon her, something changes. Her presence does not confront me directly; instead, it casts a beautiful shadow across my thoughts—soft, familiar, and impossible to ignore. It is a shadow my nature desperately tries to forget, not because it lacks beauty, but because remembering it feels dangerous. Forgetting would be easier. Forgetting would be safer. But forgetting has never been my strength.

Time and again, my nature betrays me. It speaks when I want silence, yearns when I demand restraint. It continues to express its desire in places where it is unwelcome, for people who look at me with indifference, or worse, with quiet hatred. Still, the heart persists. It does not learn from rejection; it only *deepens its voice.*

I walk forward knowing this truth—that I am both the creator of my habits and the prisoner of them. I know that my longing is self-inflicted, that my wounds carry my own fingerprints. Yet even with this awareness, I cannot stop myself from searching for her shadow in every passing moment, even when my nature knows it will never be embraced.

And so I continue—honest in my steps, conflicted in my soul—carrying desires that refuse to die, loving in directions where love was never meant to return.

There is only one rule in this world that remains painfully clear: love is like ashes.

Ashes born after a body has burned in fire, quiet and weightless, yet forever absorbed into the very place where everything once lived and breathed. Love, too, leaves behind such remains—soft, unseen, but impossible to remove.

I am like those ashes.

When I enter someone's life, I do not arrive as a storm or a flame; I arrive silently, settling into the corners of their existence. I absorb their troubles, their unrest, their unsaid fears, and in doing so, I transform myself into a fragile desire for their happiness. I become something meant to heal, meant to soothe, even when no one asks me to.

It is not necessary that I fully understand why I become this way.

Perhaps it is my nature, or perhaps it is love's cruel design. Yet this very nature troubles me endlessly. It keeps me awake in moments of silence and weighs heavily on my heart in moments meant for peace. The more I give, the more I dissolve, and with every passing moment, my pain quietly multiplies.

I remain—
Not as fire, not as warmth, but as the ashes left behind after love has done its burning. Invisible to the world, yet heavy within myself, carrying a sorrow that grows deeper precisely because it is born from love.

4

INSIDE BARS

It is not necessary that every relationship we form in this world will last until the very end. Relationships, like the weather, are subject to change. Some days they are warm and close, wrapping us in comfort; other days they grow distant, cold, and unfamiliar. People come closer when it suits their season, and when that season changes, they slowly drift away without looking back.

I believe this shifting nature of relationships is what sets me apart from many others. I do not possess the ability to detach so easily. I do not know how to loosen my grip simply because time, circumstances, or convenience demands it. When I form a bond, I carry it within me with sincerity, hoping it will endure beyond changing moods and passing phases.

Even if a relationship becomes one-sided, even if my feelings are not mirrored with the same intensity, I do not consider it meaningless.

Some connections, no matter how quiet or unreturned they may be, grow essential to our existence.

They become as necessary as breath itself—unseen, often unacknowledged, yet vital for survival. Letting go of such bonds feels less like moving on and more like losing a part of myself, *and perhaps that is my flaw, or perhaps it is my strength.*

5

BEHIND THE WAY OF HELL

What can I truly say about myself when every taunt thrown by people passes straight through me, leaving invisible marks I alone can feel? I have learned not to accept their judgments, even when they disguise them as respect. People speak as if they know me, as if they have lived my nights and carried my burdens, but their words do not define me. Still, no matter how strong my resistance is, I cannot rewrite my fate. Whatever is destined to happen will happen in its own time, and trying to separate myself from it feels like waging a silent war against God—the Supreme Being who granted me this life in the first place.

I may forget my own shadow for a moment, but fate never forgets me. It follows patiently, waiting for the right hour to return everything that is written in my share. There are paths in life so difficult that each step feels heavier than the last, roads where hope thins and courage is tested again and again. Yet even on those merciless paths, when someone close to me walks beside me, the journey becomes bearable. Their presence does not erase the pain, but it gives me strength to endure it.

In the end, I do not fight destiny, nor do I surrender to despair. I walk forward carrying faith, scars, and silence together. Because even when the world mocks me, even when fate tightens its grip, I know that having one true soul beside me can turn the hardest road into a path worth walking.

6

SCAR OF LIFE

"Relationships are not bridges to success,
for the day love becomes a path to profit,
hearts turn into marketplaces
and affection learns the language of price.
When love is used, it forgets how to stay.
When success is the goal, sincerity becomes a
casualty.
Hands are held not for warmth,
but for leverage,
and promises are spoken
only as long as they are useful.
In such love, loyalty is rented,
emotions are measured in returns,
and when the harvest ends,
the bond is abandoned like exhausted soil.
True love does not climb with you;
it walks beside you.
It does not ask what you bring,
only who you are when everything is taken away.

*Love that can be bought
was never love at all—
it was merely a bargain
waiting for its silence.*"

7

A FRAME OF LONELINESS

Even the most difficult paths begin to feel easy—not because the journey softens, but because the weight is no longer carried alone. People do not walk beside us merely because they choose to; they stay because, at some point, their needs quietly merge with ours. When two souls enter the same gathering and try to turn their natures into shadows—lowering their egos, dimming their demands—then at least one of their prayers is surely answered. I have witnessed this truth not in stories, but in life itself.

I have observed life so closely, from such a painful distance, that silence has begun to frighten me. Now, whenever silence approaches, I shut my eyes, as if darkness could protect me from it. Because if I remain fully awake within this life, it no longer feels like it belongs to me. It feels borrowed, heavy, and suffocating—like breathing inside a grave that has not yet been sealed, but already knows my name.

I have learned that living is not always about movement; sometimes it is about endurance. Sometimes it is about surviving moments where hope does not speak and faith whispers only in exhaustion. There are days when existence itself feels like a paused prayer—unfinished, unanswered—hanging somewhere between heaven and soil. And yet, even in that suspended state, something within me refuses to die. Perhaps it is habit. Perhaps it is belief. Or perhaps it is the quiet understanding that even graves are not the end, only a place where silence learns how to wait.

8
KEEP PROMISES

❦

Every one of its names carries meaning, and each is undeniably deserved. Yet there is one truth that remains unchanged through every story and every life: never lose yourself for the sake of someone else. The moment you do, two quiet catastrophes begin to unfold. The first is the loss of your own identity—slow, invisible, but devastating. The second is even crueler: you begin to see yourself as weak, as if your worth has somehow diminished because you chose to disappear inside another person's existence.

In that fragile state, the heart and the mind stop speaking the same language. You stand trapped between what you feel and what you know, unable to choose either without betraying yourself. Thoughts collide, emotions overflow, and the world around you starts to blur, as though reality itself has lost its edges. What once felt clear now feels distant, unreachable.

Confidence, which once stood firm within you, begins to crack without warning. It shatters silently, leaving behind doubts you never invited. You question your decisions, your strength, even your right to want more. Slowly, the world stretches out before you like a vast, restless ocean—endless and overwhelming—where every direction looks the same, and hope feels like an illusion shimmering just beyond reach.

In that ocean, life no longer feels solid. It becomes a mirage: beautiful from afar, but impossible to hold. And only then do you realize that losing yourself for someone else is not love—it is the quiet erasure of everything you once were.

9
BLUR MEMORIES

"*I am starting to lose myself nowadays, I am a destination, I am starting to find a way in myself and if you know me better then tell me in which streets I am growing up nowadays.*"

10
WELL BUT FORGET

The thirst will be quenched one day, yes—but even then, fate will still come asking for its due. It will ask at a time when you will have already given away everything that once belonged to him, when all his customs, habits, and memories will have been unknowingly mixed into your own share of life.

I am only eighteen years old, yet in these few passing days, I have lived the weight of a hundred years. Time has aged me in silence. I am that person who has been betrayed only in love, not once, but in ways that leave invisible scars. I am that person who, no matter which direction he looks, sees nothing but destruction written into his fate—as if ruin has memorized my address.

There was a time when I truly believed God had gifted me a beautiful life. I walked with gratitude, trusting that goodness was permanent. But slowly, painfully, I understood something else: when nothing seems to go wrong, when life flows too smoothly, that itself becomes the imbalance. That comfort, that illusion of safety, quietly prepares the fall.

Today, I stand alone—with no one but myself. And the truth is heavier than loneliness: I am not defeated by the world, I am defeated by my own self. I possess the strength to become exactly what I once tried a thousand times to stay away from. I fought it, resisted it, escaped it—yet in the end, my fate turned me in the same direction. As if destiny enjoys irony.

There are thoughts inside me that do not allow me to live peacefully. They haunt me relentlessly, as though they were never truly mine, yet they refuse to leave. They disturb my nights, poison my silence, and question my existence. I no longer recognize myself the way I used to. I feel fragmented, scattered across moments I never chose.

And when I cannot remain true to myself, when I cannot even hold onto who I am—then what hope do I have of becoming something meaningful for someone else in the future?

11

THE LESSON OF LIFE

—❦—

Human relationships in this world are rarely worthy of complete trust. What begins with warmth and promises often fades under the weight of selfish needs, unspoken expectations, and quiet betrayals. People walk beside us for a while, sharing laughter, secrets, and dreams, yet the moment circumstances change, many turn away as if those moments never existed. Trust, once broken, does not shatter loudly—it erodes silently, grain by grain, until one day we realize that what we were standing on was never solid ground.

In this world, relationships are often shaped by convenience rather than commitment. Affection survives only as long as it is beneficial, and loyalty is tested the moment sacrifice is required. Words are spoken with ease, but intentions remain hidden behind polite smiles. The hardest truth is not that people change, but that they reveal who they were all along when loyalty becomes inconvenient.

And so, one learns that while relationships may offer comfort, they should never become the sole foundation of one's strength. In a world where trust is fragile and promises are temporary, the only bond that must remain unbroken is the one we build with ourselves—steady, honest, and strong enough to endure when all others fail.

12
FAR FROM SUNSHINE

Every image I try to imagine of my future arrives like a long, trembling shadow of ruin. It does not frighten me anymore; fear would at least mean I still had something left to protect. What I feel now is exhaustion—an exhaustion that has nothing to do with age and everything to do with burden. It is the weariness of belonging to a community that keeps demanding its share of me, again and again, until there is hardly anything left to give.

They take not only my time or my strength, but my silence, my patience, and my memories. It feels as though every step forward requires a sacrifice, and every sacrifice costs me a piece of myself. Just yesterday, a bitter thought crossed my mind—that perhaps I should hate the people who forced me to erase every memory connected to my happiness. Perhaps hatred would be easier. Perhaps it would give shape to this hollow ache.

But it does not happen that way.

Hatred demands energy, and I no longer have enough of it to waste. Instead of anger, there is only a quiet, suffocating sadness. The memories they tried to erase still linger, not as joy, but as distant echoes—faint reminders of a life that once felt lighter, freer, and mine. I did not lose those moments because they were meaningless; I lost them because they mattered too much.

So I walk forward, not broken, not afraid, but tired in a way that words struggle to carry. Tired of giving explanations. Tired of defending my right to exist as myself. Tired of being told that my happiness must always come second to expectations, traditions, and unspoken rules.

And yet, despite everything, I cannot bring myself to hate. Because even in this exhaustion, somewhere beneath the weight of loss and responsibility, I still remember who I was before they asked me to forget—and that memory, however fragile, refuses to die.

13

COMPLEX U-TURN

If you ever fall in love with someone, understand this first: love does not always give you the right to interfere, to fix, or to carry every wound they hide within themselves. Do not force them to feel something they are not ready to feel. Do not insist on understanding every layer of their pain, and do not try to make all of their problems your own burden to carry.

There are battles in a person's life that no love, no presence, and no sacrifice can solve. And sometimes, deep down, you already know the truth—you know that no matter how much you care, you cannot change their reality or ease their suffering. When that clarity arrives, holding on is no longer an act of love; it becomes an act of quiet self-destruction.

In such moments, the bravest thing you can do is step back. Leave them where they are, not because you never cared, but because you cared enough to understand your limits. Control your heart, gather the scattered pieces of your thoughts, and choose to move forward, even when every part of you wants to stay.

Stop asking questions that only reopen wounds. Stop searching for reasons that will never bring peace. Instead, give yourself one honest answer: I want to move ahead. I do not want to remain trapped in memories or thoughts that only grow stronger and heavier with time. I choose distance over despair, acceptance over endless hope, and progress over emotional exhaustion.

Because sometimes, loving someone also means knowing when to let go—and loving yourself enough to walk away.

14

LET MY SOUL

They say it will make me weak, but weakness is not the issue here, sir—it is a matter of capacity. Life does not move according to our comfort. The wind does not always blow in our favor, carrying with it treasures of happiness and ease. There are days when it lifts us high, and there are nights when it stands still, refusing to move at all.

And when, by some rare mercy, life begins to feel happy, that is when caution becomes necessary. One must first step away from the very people who are making that happiness visible. Because happiness, when exposed too openly, invites betrayal. If you express love in front of them, they will one day use it as a weapon against you. And if you choose silence or show even a trace of hatred, society will place its weight upon your chest, questioning your character, your intentions, your existence.

Trapped between love and resentment, approval and judgment, we reach a moment where nothing seems right. Every path feels wrong, every decision feels dangerous. At that time, we sit quietly and ask ourselves—what are we supposed to do when there is nothing left to be done?

And then a deeper question rises, heavier than the rest: why do we even think so much in moments like these? Perhaps because thinking is the last refuge of a heart that has nowhere else to go. When actions fail us, thoughts become our battlefield. We fight ourselves in silence, searching for meaning in confusion, strength in stillness, and answers in questions that may never be resolved.

That is not weakness. That is endurance. That is the capacity to survive when the wind no longer blows, and all we are left with is ourselves.

15
REVENGE BEHIND ADORE

What will they say, and what will they do? These questions often haunt us more than reality itself. Yet if we are truly happy in our own world, why should we feel the need to seek approval from any other world? And if our world is distant from happiness, then shouldn't we work to make it better instead of surrendering to despair?

Rather than constantly presenting ourselves as portraits of sorrow, we must remember that we have been given only one world, one life, and one chance to exist as ourselves. When you arrive in this world, you are faced with a simple but powerful choice: live it with laughter, courage, and hope, or burden yourself by stretching your sorrow so long that it begins to consume your peace.

Pain will come, and hardships will test us, but choosing to multiply our grief only steals the life we still have. Worrying endlessly about others' opinions builds a prison of invisible walls, where peace cannot survive. Happiness does not come from escaping into another world; it is created when we dare to heal the one we already live in.

In the end, life does not ask us to be perfect—it asks us to be alive. To breathe through the pain, to smile despite the scars, and to choose joy even when sorrow stands close. Because this world is the only one we truly own, and how we live in it will decide whether we merely exist or truly live.

16

RUN

Sometimes, in the quiet urgency of taking care of everyone else, we slowly forget ourselves. We become so occupied with mending broken days, easing other people's pain, and standing strong for those who lean on us, that we neglect the fragile space within our own hearts. In doing so, we unknowingly hand over the most delicate part of ourselves to the wind—trusting it to carry our feelings safely to where they belong.

But the wind is careless. Instead of guiding our heart toward understanding or peace, it drifts away, lost in directions we never intended. What was meant to become light turns into distance, and what we hoped would heal us begins to unravel. Gradually, without realizing when it began, we find ourselves surrounded by a darkness that does not arrive suddenly, but settles in quietly, layer by layer.

This darkness is not loud or dramatic; it is heavy and persistent. It clouds our thoughts, weakens our strength, and makes even familiar paths feel unfamiliar. And the most painful part is that once we are trapped inside it, escaping becomes difficult—not because there is no way out, but because we are too exhausted to search for one. We gave so much of ourselves away that when the time comes to save our own soul, we no longer know where to begin.

17

SECRET

❦

"*If I fall, who will pick me up?*
If I lose my temper, who will hold me up?
And I will kill myself to have you.
But who will tell me this secret after I die?"

18
COWARD

I have tried, every single time, to walk with caution—to measure my steps, to think before I fall. Yet now, life no longer feels as simple as I once believed it to be. The paths I imagined as straight have twisted into corridors of doubt, and every choice carries the weight of consequences I never anticipated. Still, no matter how heavy this burden becomes, I cannot allow myself to accept defeat.

Because the moment I surrender, I know what I will turn into—a coward, not in the eyes of the world, but in my own. And that is a judgment far harsher than any failure life could hand me. I have seen what cowardice does; it grows silently, becomes a habit, and slowly eats away at the soul. I refuse to let that habit take root in me, because I know it would ruin whatever remains of who I am.

I say this with painful honesty: I have already ruined myself many times, in my own ways, through my own choices. I have broken my own trust, disappointed my own reflection, and stood amid the wreckage of decisions I cannot undo. But perhaps that is precisely why I stand here now—still breathing, still thinking, still fighting. Maybe this is the moment where weakening myself is no longer necessary, especially for those *who could never truly become my own.*

I have spent enough strength trying to belong where I was never meant to stay. I have bent, endured, and bled silently for people who never looked back. And now I understand—my strength should not be wasted on those who do not see my worth.

I have seen darker days than these. I have walked through nights that felt endless, carried pain that words could not hold, and survived storms that should have broken me completely. Compared to those moments, this struggle is not the end—it is only another test. And as long as I remember what I have already survived, I know I am not finished yet.

I may be tired, and I may be wounded, but I am not defeated.

19

WHO KNOW ME?

If I touch them, I can pull myself away from them. The distance is possible—at least in theory. All I have to do is admit one simple truth to myself: that I need them. But that admission feels heavier than separation itself, so I avoid it. I pretend strength where there is hesitation, and independence where there is fear.

I have never truly understood what I want from my life. That is the most confusing part. I have everything that is required to live—a roof, time, breath, opportunities, even people who care. On paper, my life is complete. And yet, somewhere deep inside, I feel hollow. I call myself weak, not because the world has defeated me, but because I am quietly destroying myself for something I already understand far too well.

The painful irony is this: I know exactly what that "something" is. I can name it. I can see it. I can feel its weight every single day. And still, I cannot separate myself from it. It has wrapped itself around my thoughts so tightly that even when I try to walk away, I carry it with me. I blame it for my suffering, yet I cling to it as if letting go would leave me with nothing at all.

Sometimes it feels as though my life has paused at a certain moment—a single invisible point in time where everything stopped moving forward. The world continues, people grow, days pass, but I remain there, standing still. No matter how much I want to move ahead, my feet refuse to follow my will. I am not falling backward, nor am I progressing forward; I am simply stuck, suspended between what I was and what I could become.

And perhaps the hardest part is knowing that the prison I am trapped in has no locked door—only one I am afraid to open.

20
BECOME MY SLAVE

Even though I am fully aware of the dynamics of every relationship in my life, I often find myself neglecting my own needs and well-being. It's not that I don't value myself, but rather that I place so much importance on these bonds that I constantly prioritize them over my own happiness. I invest my energy, my time, and my emotions into making others happy, even if it means sacrificing pieces of myself in the process. And yet, if these relationships were not important to me, I wouldn't feel this intense tug between giving and losing; I wouldn't feel the weight of responsibility to uphold someone else's joy.

I find myself longing for a day when I can truly return to myself—a day when I can exist without relying on anyone's affection, approval, or presence. A day when I can simply breathe and live, free from the constant push and pull of others' expectations. I wish I could be complete in my own solitude, drawing strength only from within, without the need to tether my happiness to anyone else.

The struggle is real. On one hand, my mind is filled with anxiety about the future, about the uncertain paths that lie ahead, and the responsibilities I cannot escape. On the other hand, there's a burning desire within me to keep moving forward, to grow, to evolve, and to claim my own space in the world. Yes, I have grown—sometimes in small, hesitant steps, sometimes with trembling confidence—but growth is growth, no matter how fragile or slow.

But this does not mean that I should become a servant to the expectations of others, nor that my efforts should be bound entirely to keeping others content. I am not meant to lose myself entirely in the service of anyone else. I long for balance, for a life where my own heart matters as much as the hearts I care for. I long for a moment when I can finally reclaim myself, when I can embrace both my fears and my desires without guilt or hesitation, and when I can walk forward in life with the quiet, unshakable certainty that my happiness does not need to depend on anyone else.

21

OLD ETCHED

❦

Well, every story has a story behind it, just as every sorrow hides a glimpse of someone's essence within it. In much the same way, my beginning was shaped by moments that were both unique and deeply personal, moments that carried the weight of memory yet shimmered with the promise of something original. I have always sought something that is entirely my own—something no one else can claim or fully understand.

The memories I carry are old, etched into the folds of my mind, yet they do not define me completely. People may have seen fragments of my nature, may have glimpsed parts of who I am, but my true self—the core of my being—remains known only to me. It is a private compass, a quiet strength that I carry silently through the world.

Even when challenges arise or troubles attempt to claim a piece of me, they cannot break me. They may knock at my door, they may try to sway me, but the essence I guard so carefully is mine alone. It is a force, a presence, a truth that anchors me. And as long as it remains with me, it is both a shield and a guide—a part of me that may bring occasional struggle but will never bring surrender.

What is this, then, that I hold so dearly? It is the intimate knowledge of myself—my nature, my spirit, my untold story. It is the seed of resilience, the unseen flame, the quiet certainty that no matter what comes, I remain unshaken, because I alone carry its light.

22

PARADOX OF LOVE

The only real advice I can give about love is this: if your feelings for someone are genuine and you are thinking of building a relationship, first take the time to truly understand yourself and the nature of your emotions. Love is not a game to be rushed. Hasty decisions, impulsive actions, or trying to force connections often lead not only to heartbreak but also to a deeper kind of personal suffering. Relationships are fragile, yes, but even more fragile is the human heart that invests itself in them.

There is no rule in this world that says love must be acted upon immediately, or that you must sacrifice your own well-being to keep someone close. Before thinking about what the other person might feel or expect, care for yourself. Your emotions, your stability, and your sense of self are the foundations upon which any healthy relationship can stand. Often, we imagine that after we leave someone's life, everything will change—people will feel our absence, circumstances will shift, and somehow, the world will acknowledge our importance. But the truth is, life rarely bends to our expectations. Neither will others change simply because we wish it, nor should we alter our own nature to fit into someone else's world.

This is the paradox of love: it asks us to give, yet it demands self-awareness; it invites surrender, yet it requires a strong sense of self. Real love does not pressure you. It does not demand that you lose yourself to prove your feelings. Love, at its purest, is a choice you make with clarity, patience, and respect—for both yourself and the other person. Understand this first, and everything else—the joy, the heartbreak, the growth—will follow naturally.

23

ALONE PATH

Whoever you are, whoever you aspire to become, remain true to your own path. You do not need to rely on anyone else to validate your existence, nor should you let others' presence dilute your strength. Sometimes, in our desire for companionship or approval, we bring people close to us, believing they make us stronger—but often, it is the opposite. Instead of uplifting us, they quietly weaken our resolve, cloud our judgment, and stir doubts within us that were never there before.

The real power lies not in others, but within yourself. Hold your own hand firmly, face the shadows that dwell inside, and confront every fear, every insecurity, every whisper of negativity that tries to take root in your mind. Tell them firmly: I do not need you. You are enough on your own.

Ironically, those we sometimes wish to avoid or distance ourselves from can become, in their absence, the catalysts of our inner strength. The very people or circumstances that challenge us, frustrate us, or attempt to hold us back can teach us resilience, patience, and courage—if only we stand firm and refuse to let them control our spirit.

So walk your path alone if you must. Nurture yourself. Cleanse your soul of negativity. Guard your energy fiercely. Because true strength is not borrowed—it is grown, nurtured, and claimed from within. And when you finally recognize this, you realize that the power to rise, to heal, and to thrive has always been in your hands.

24

INTRUDERS

That silence will not disturb you as much as the silence of an empty, open room does. A room that echoes with your own breathing, where every thought returns to you louder than before, where even memories begin to feel like intruders. Silence, when shared, can be gentle—but when it surrounds you alone, it becomes heavy, almost unbearable.

If you already know about yourself that you cannot handle it, then at least stop it. Stop it before it consumes you, and stop them before they slowly ruin you. Because with time, those very things you once ignored grow stronger, more demanding, and far more merciless. At first, they seem harmless, almost invisible, but gradually they tighten their grip until you feel helpless, trapped inside your own mind, unable to escape their constant pressure.

I am not capable enough to tell you my problem openly. It is tied to my life so deeply that words fail me every time I try to explain it. There are truths I carry that remain unspoken—not because I do not wish to share them, but because I do not know how. What can I do, after all? My life has given me happiness in proportion to my pain, and sometimes even more pain than joy. Yet that balance, however cruel, has stitched my yesterday to my today.

Every wound I carry reminds me of where I have been, and every small moment of happiness reminds me that I survived. The past refuses to loosen its hold, and the present keeps demanding strength I am not sure I possess. Still, I move forward, carrying both joy and suffering together, because they are inseparable now. They are the silent witnesses of my journey, binding my memories, my losses, and my hopes into a single, fragile existence.

25

DOORWAY

Life often presents itself as a doorway to a new beginning, a path leading toward a future filled with endless possibilities. Someone once said that life exists for the purpose of learning, for accumulating wisdom through experience. Yet, as I stand here now, I find myself questioning that notion. Do we truly learn at every moment, or do we only learn when life demands it of us, when circumstances force us into the classroom of reality? Perhaps learning is not a continuous journey but a series of urgent lessons, each one appearing precisely when we need it the most.

If the universe has already woven guidance and preparation into the very fabric of our existence, then why does it still seem necessary for us to stumble, to falter, and to struggle in order to understand? Perhaps the answer is not in seeking knowledge externally, but in strengthening the core of our being—our resilience, our spirit, our capacity to endure. When we make ourselves strong enough, the chaos of the world, the restless silence of uncertainty, and the shadows of doubt no longer intimidate us. Instead, they transform into the first whispers of genuine happiness—a quiet, profound joy that arises from within, untouched by circumstance.

True strength, then, is not just the ability to survive the storms, but the courage to embrace silence, to meet solitude without fear, and to discover that happiness often begins not in noise or excitement, but in the calm acceptance of life as it is. In that serene strength, every pause, every shadow, every moment of stillness becomes a teacher, and every silence becomes the doorway to a brighter, more meaningful future.

26
FRAGMENTS

—♡—

Whatever I try to write today, I fear that his picture will never come out clearly. Perhaps that's because his story is unfinished, like a book with missing chapters, like a melody that stops abruptly before it finds its resolution. He has never truly been complete—not in the way one dreams of completeness—because his dreams, too, were left unfinished, suspended somewhere between hope and reality.

Life with him has always been a pattern of meetings and departures. We meet, we speak, we laugh, we share fragments of our thoughts, and then we part ways—only to meet again, repeat the same dance of conversation and silence. It leaves me wondering: is this what life is meant to be? A series of incomplete encounters, fleeting moments that promise connection but never fully deliver?

I find myself questioning everything I once thought I knew about myself. In posing these questions, I realize I only truly understood myself in the act of wondering about him. But now... now I feel lost, as if even the reflection I once trusted has become distorted. Whatever I am trying to express may not be understood by everyone—and perhaps that's the nature of it. Those who might understand today may not comprehend tomorrow, because life, emotions, and human connections are far more intricate than words can capture.

Maybe this is life: a puzzle with pieces that never seem to fit, a labyrinth of fleeting encounters, unfinished dreams, and questions that echo endlessly without clear answers. And yet, even in the uncertainty, even in the incompleteness, there is something undeniably profound—a quiet longing that insists on being felt, even if it cannot be fully explained.

27

INTRICATE PUZZLE

First of all, remember this: life, in its essence, is like a vast, intricate puzzle. For most of us, it remains confusing, a maze of questions and uncertainties, until there comes someone who can guide us, who can help us make sense of the chaos. Until that moment arrives, life can feel fragmented, as if the pieces will never fit together.

Life becomes particularly puzzling when the people you once held close begin to drift away. When friends stop calling, when conversations that once felt effortless and comforting start to fade into silence, when the very people you trusted start turning their backs—it's in these moments that life begins to feel heavy, complicated, almost unsolvable. And nothing magnifies that sense of emptiness more than when someone you love, someone who occupies a space in your heart larger than yourself, walks away. In that absence, life doesn't just feel incomplete—it feels like a puzzle missing its most crucial piece, a riddle with no answer, a melody without harmony.

Then there are the dreams you once held so dearly. The dreams that burned brightly in your heart, that gave you purpose and direction, that you believed were your destiny. When they remain unfulfilled, or worse, when they slowly slip away despite your tireless efforts, sorrow seeps in quietly, insidiously. Life, in such moments, doesn't just feel like a puzzle—it feels like a heavy, unrelenting storm of disappointment, loss, and unanswered questions. The world can seem colder, emptier, and the path forward more uncertain than ever.

Yet, even amidst all this confusion and heartache, there is a subtle, almost invisible hope. For every puzzle has its solution, even if it takes time to see. Every loss, every setback, every moment of silence is teaching you something, shaping you, preparing you to understand life more deeply. And perhaps, one day, when the pieces finally fall into place, when clarity arrives in the form of understanding, love, or self-realization, the puzzle will make sense—and life, in all its chaos and beauty, will finally feel complete.

28
MYSTERY

—♡—

There are countless things to say and an endless spectrum of emotions to feel, yet one must pause and wonder—are these truly ours? When we speak of others, when we frame our thoughts in words about someone else, are those thoughts genuinely born from our own mind, or are they mere echoes of what we have absorbed from the world around us? Life often presents us with paths that seem clear, paths that stretch far beyond the horizon. The way may be smooth and the direction obvious, yet the destination remains distant, shrouded in uncertainty. And even when thirst gnaws at our spirit, when longing and desire cling to every step, life can begin to feel heavy, almost as if it were a burden rather than a blessing.

We often find ourselves trapped in the labyrinth of time—questioning what we did in the past, regretting choices that have already been made, or imagining roads not taken. And yet, why should the past hold us prisoner when it is nothing more than a shadow of what has already happened? Similarly, why should the future, uncertain and untamed, stir fear within us, when it is only a canvas waiting for the brushstrokes of our present actions? The present is the only moment we truly possess, yet even here, we hesitate. We hold back words, unsaid feelings, and gestures of love or apology, thinking that timing must be perfect, that circumstances must align.

But why? If the heart wishes to speak, if the soul longs to express itself, then no clock, no calendar, no moment of convenience can dictate its urgency. Time is not the master of truth, nor is it the keeper of connection. Every moment we delay is a moment lost, a chance slipping silently into the void. Life, in all its vastness and mystery, urges us to speak, to act, to feel—not tomorrow, not yesterday, but now. And perhaps in embracing the present fully, in surrendering the weight of past and future, we find a clarity, a freedom, a sense of life that is no longer a burden, but a journey worth traveling, step by step, word by word, feeling by feeling.

29

FRAGILE VESSEL

<p>

Everyone knows that hearts are delicate, fragile vessels that can shatter with the slightest blow. But what most fail to realize is that when hearts break, they do not always remain tender; sometimes, they harden, turning into something as unyielding as stone. Time, as merciless as it is patient, shapes everything—it changes the world, the seasons, the winds, and even the currents of rivers. Yet, in the vast, subtle workings of time, people often forget that humans too are not exempt from this relentless transformation.

I have witnessed it with my own eyes—the slow, almost imperceptible shift in a person's nature, the gradual molding of their thoughts, desires, and even their identity. And what is most astonishing is that these changes are rarely for the sake of others. People evolve, adapt, and sometimes harden purely for themselves, guided by their own experiences, pains, and the lessons life forces upon them.

It is a curious, almost unsettling phenomenon: someone you once knew intimately, whose laughter and dreams were familiar, can grow into a version of themselves that feels entirely alien. Their priorities shift, their reactions transform, and their very essence seems to drift into unrecognizable territory. At times, it is as if the person you loved or understood has not merely changed but has been reborn into a being whose presence challenges your memory of them, whose very identity becomes a puzzle that even you cannot solve.

And in witnessing this, one learns a profound truth: people change not because the world demands it of them, nor because others need them to, but because life itself, with its relentless currents, reshapes them in ways both beautiful and unsettling. To see someone change for themselves is to confront the fragile, stone-hard paradox of the human heart—a vessel that can break, harden, and yet still beat, still carry the weight of memory, hope, and the inexorable march of time.

30
IRONY

As much as this world seems broken and marred by chaos, there are always people who are willing to sacrifice every aspect of themselves to exploit that very brokenness. They twist and corrupt what is pure, and yet, paradoxically, society applauds them, considers their cunning as wisdom, and eventually embraces them as one of its own. The irony is bitter—those who trade their integrity for gain are often the ones celebrated, while those who strive to protect or heal are overlooked or even condemned.

This world, in its essence, is like a mother—boundless, nurturing, and forgiving—but often we approach it with the weight of superstitions, blind beliefs, and inherited prejudices, seeing the world not as it is but as a reflection of the relationships, rules, and fears we have been taught to honor. We claim to respect it, yet our actions betray it, leaving scars that future generations must bear.

Promises—oh, the fragile and fleeting promises we make! We utter them not only in love, friendship, or familial bonds, but also to ourselves. We swear to change, to rise, to pursue dreams, or to correct our flaws. Yet, when the moment comes to fulfill them, we forget. We show off the very act of remembering as if that alone honors the promise. Perhaps this is the cruel paradox of human nature: we take years to cultivate goodness, patience, and discipline, but bad habits, vices, and neglect are learned with astonishing speed, spreading and rooting themselves effortlessly within us.

Even today, I struggle to understand why we forget what we promise, why the path to virtue seems long and arduous while the descent into error is swift and inviting. Maybe it is the way the world teaches us, maybe it is the weakness within ourselves, or maybe it is simply the inevitability of human imperfection. And yet, despite all this, we continue—making promises, breaking them, hurting, forgiving, learning, and forgetting—bound in an endless cycle of hope and failure, love and loss, illusion and awakening.

31
KNEEDEEP

They do—often far too quickly.

I can speak these words in my own voice because I have lived through more than enough time to understand them. I have endured seasons that bent me, moments that hollowed me out, and silences that spoke louder than screams. I have watched people at their weakest—standing knee-deep in water as they gathered what little they could save, their reflections trembling with uncertainty. In those moments, I did not just see them; I saw myself.

Somewhere along the way, I realized that they were breaking apart—not because they were weak, but because they were breaking for someone else. Piece by piece, quietly, without complaint. I know that fracture well, because it once lived inside me too. I have stood in the same place, sacrificing parts of myself for reasons I could not fully explain at the time.

I carry a story of my own, one that is tangled like a puzzle with missing pieces. Certain doors in that story remain closed, and some rooms behind them are empty—echoing with things that were never said, never finished, never healed. Even today, those empty spaces call out to me. They ask to be remembered, to be acknowledged, to be spoken into existence.

Today, I feel the need to open those doors, even if only a little. I want to speak what has been buried for years. I want to express every memory tied to my past—the faces, the moments, the fractures, and the quiet strength hidden beneath them. Not to rewrite what happened, but to finally let it breathe.

Because some stories do not fade with time. They wait. And today, I am ready to tell mine.

32

ONE LIFE

I had never spoken about this to anyone in my entire life—not because I was hiding it, but because there was never a moment when I felt I truly had to say it. For a long time, people kept asking me the same question in different ways: What is it that you want to do with your life? What do you really want?

Their voices echoed around me, but I remained silent. While the world was busy questioning me, I was quietly creating my own memories—memories born in solitude, in unspoken pain, in those silent abuses that leave no visible scars but carve themselves deep into the soul. At that time, I was young, unaware, and painfully naïve, yet somewhere inside me, I understood one thing very clearly.

I never wanted to be known as the son of a powerful or wealthy father. I never wished to stand in front of people and prove that I had more than them—more money, more influence, more privilege. That kind of comparison never interested me. I did not want borrowed pride or inherited respect. I wanted to exist on my own terms, even if that meant standing alone.

In those quiet years, when no one was watching and no one was listening, I was learning how to endure. I was learning how to live without asking for validation, how to carry my worth without displaying it like a badge. I didn't want applause; I wanted peace. I didn't want to dominate others; I wanted to understand myself.

So when people asked me what I had to do, what I planned to become, I had no simple answer. Not because I was lost, but because my journey was inward before it could ever be outward. I was building something invisible—my character, my resilience, my silence. And perhaps that was the bravest thing I could do at that time: to grow quietly, without proving anything to anyone.

33

TIME IS A MIRAGE — THE ETERNAL NOW

Time is a river that seems to flow, carrying all moments from past to future. Yet when you pause, when you look deeply, you realize that this flow is an illusion. The past exists only in memory, fragile and distorted. The future exists only in imagination, uncertain and unreal. Only the present truly exists—and even it is fleeting, a spark that disappears as soon as it is noticed.

We live as if we are prisoners of time, yet we are not. We measure our lives in hours, days, and years, as if they were solid, tangible things. But the clock ticks only to remind the mind of its own illusions. Every second, every breath, every heartbeat is both here and gone simultaneously. To cling to it is to grasp at smoke. To resist it is to struggle with the wind.

TO BE LOST BUT ALIVE IS TO DANCE WITH TIME WITHOUT EVER TOUCHING IT.

Imagine standing on the shore of a vast, endless ocean. Waves come and go, rising and falling, each unique, yet none permanent. Time is like these waves. Each moment arises, does its work, and disappears, leaving behind only the eternal sea beneath. You cannot hold the wave, nor can you stop it—but you can float on its surface, aware of the depth beneath, untouched by its passing.

The mind craves continuity. It fears endings and longs for beginnings. It mourns what is gone and dreams of what might come. But in the awareness of the present, time collapses. There is no before, no after—only the eternal now. Every moment is complete, perfect, infinite in its own fleeting existence.

To live fully, one must see through the illusion of time. Life is not a line to be crossed, nor a ladder to be climbed. Life is a series of sparks, each illuminating the eternal space in which they appear. When the illusion of linear progression fades, there is freedom. There is no regret for the past, no anxiety for the future—only the vibrant, living pulse of now.

The eternal now is not passive. It is alive. It breathes in every movement, every sensation, every thought. To exist in this moment is to recognize that life does not belong to the clock, the calendar, or the mind. It belongs to the awareness that perceives it—silent, vast, and free.

TIME IS A MIRAGE. ONLY NOW IS REAL. BE LOST IN IT, AND YOU WILL BE TRULY ALIVE.

34

PEAC ARISE

The mind is an endless storyteller. It spins webs of memory, desire, fear, and imagination, creating the illusion of continuity, identity, and control. Thoughts rise and fall like sparks in the night, bright for a moment, then fading into nothingness. Yet we cling to them as if they define who we are, as if they hold the key to happiness, safety, and truth.

To be lost but alive is to observe the mind without becoming entangled in its stories. Thoughts are like passing clouds, drifting across the sky of awareness. They may darken the day, bring shade, or momentary rain, but the sky itself remains vast, open, and untouched. When we watch thoughts with detached curiosity, we begin to see their fleeting nature. No single thought can imprison the infinite space of consciousness that witnesses it.

The mind creates illusions of past and future, weaving them into patterns of regret, longing, and anxiety. Yet these illusions have no real substance. They are shadows projected on the walls of awareness, never permanent, never solid. By observing without attachment, we begin to notice the silence between thoughts—the stillness that underlies every movement of the mind.

Every emotion, every urge, every mental image appears and disappears, leaving the awareness unaffected. This is the door to freedom. To recognize the impermanence of thought is to stop being swept away by it. The mind may chatter endlessly, but it cannot disturb the observer who has awakened to its transience.

Meditate on the nature of a single thought. Watch it arise, examine it, and let it pass. Observe another. And another. With each, notice the gap between, the silent, ever-present awareness. It is here, in this quiet observation, that the mind's illusions dissolve. Here, the observer discovers that life is not dictated by thought, but experienced through the spaciousness in which thought moves.

Peace is not the absence of thoughts, but the recognition that you are not your thoughts. You are the awareness in which they appear and vanish. Lost but alive, you remain untouched, calm, and vast, witnessing the endless play of the mind without grasping, resisting, or judging.

The mind will continue to spin its stories. But when awareness awakens, you see them for what they are—fleeting shadows on the surface of consciousness. And in seeing, you are free.

THE MIND IS A STREAM OF ILLUSIONS. WITNESS IT WITHOUT ATTACHMENT, AND PEACE WILL ARISE.

35

FLEETING

Sorrow and joy appear as opposites, yet both are fleeting, temporary ripples on the same infinite ocean of being. Sorrow seems heavy, pressing against the chest, bending the spirit, while joy feels light, lifting the heart with its bright, effervescent glow. Yet both arise and vanish, coming and going as naturally as the tide. Neither lasts, neither defines, neither claims the essence beneath.

To be lost but alive is to witness these waves without being carried away. Let sorrow wash over you, its weight felt, its lessons absorbed, yet without attachment. Let joy bloom within you, radiating warmth, yet without grasping. Both are experiences, passing forms in the eternal space of awareness. Neither diminishes nor completes the vast presence that watches.

Every emotion carries its own color, its own vibration. Anguish may seem endless, ecstasy may seem infinite, but in the grand stillness beyond perception, they are mere shadows—reflections in a mirror of consciousness. By observing without clinging, without fear, we awaken to a deeper freedom. The heart no longer resists the rhythm of life; it flows with it.

Life itself is a dance of contrasts. Darkness and light, birth and death, loss and gain, pain and pleasure—all move together in intricate patterns, inseparable yet distinct. When we stop identifying with one side of the dance, when we stop judging one as good and another as bad, we find peace. We become the quiet space in which the dance unfolds, untouched and eternal.

Sorrow teaches; joy inspires. Neither is permanent, yet both are meaningful when seen without attachment. Like waves on the ocean, they rise, crest, fall, and vanish, leaving the sea unchanged. Awareness does the same with emotions—it notices, feels, and releases, resting in the depth that is beyond all form.

To live fully in this awareness is to be free. To be lost but alive is to experience life in its fullness without needing to cling or flee, to understand that the highs and lows are but passing ripples, and to rest in the quiet, eternal presence that underlies them all.

SORROW AND JOY ARE WAVES. FLOAT ON THEM WITHOUT ATTACHMENT, AND YOU WILL DISCOVER TRUE FREEDOM.

36
WHISTLE

The world hums with ceaseless noise. Voices chatter, machines roar, winds whistle, hearts beat, and thoughts swirl endlessly. Yet beneath all this movement lies a silence that is absolute, eternal, and untouched. It is not a sound, nor an absence of sound—it simply is. It is the unchanging essence in which all forms appear and disappear.

To be lost but alive is to notice this silence, to dwell within it even while the world moves in chaos. The clamor of life does not disturb it; it remains vast and calm, a silent ocean beneath the waves. In this awareness, you realize that the noise of the world is only the surface, temporary and shifting, while the stillness beneath is permanent, infinite, and serene.

Silence is not emptiness. It is fullness beyond form. Within it, thoughts settle, emotions calm, and the mind rests. Every sound, every movement, every sensation can be experienced fully, without attachment, because the observer resides in the quiet that watches it all. In this space, there is no fear, no longing, no need for anything to be other than it is.

Imagine a forest at dawn. Birds sing, leaves rustle, a stream flows, yet amidst it all, there is a quiet that permeates every sound—a stillness that holds all movement without being affected. This is the silence beyond sound, the eternal presence that watches the world without clinging or judgment.

To live in this silence is to live fully. To hear it is to awaken. It is a reminder that life's noise, with all its distractions and illusions, cannot disturb the heart that has found its anchor in stillness. The waves of sound and activity may rise, but they do not touch the depth beneath.

Being lost but alive is to dwell in this awareness. You notice the world, feel the sensations, and move with life, yet remain untouched by its noise. Silence becomes your companion, your teacher, your home. Here, every moment is complete. Every breath is a meditation. Every heartbeat is a hymn to the eternal now.

SILENCE IS THE UNDERLYING REALITY. HEAR IT, DWELL IN IT, AND YOU WILL BE TRULY FREE.

37

TRUE FREEDOM

Freedom is not found in changing the world. It is not earned through achievement, nor discovered in places or possessions. True freedom arises when the illusions of the mind dissolve, when the veil of appearances lifts, and awareness sees clearly. To be lost but alive is to awaken to this truth: that life continues in its flow, yet the observer remains untouched, calm, and infinite.

We spend so much of existence chasing control, fearing loss, and clinging to permanence. Yet all of these are illusions, constructs of thought that obscure the vast presence beneath. Liberation begins when we stop resisting what is, when we stop trying to hold or shape the world, and instead rest in awareness itself.

In awareness, life is neither burden nor reward. It simply is. Each moment is a spark of experience, neither good nor bad, neither lasting nor fleeting. The observer witnesses all without attachment, without judgment, without need. The heart that rests in this awareness experiences peace that is unshakable, a calm that cannot be disturbed by the waves of life.

To awaken is not to escape, but to move with life fully and freely. The currents of joy, sorrow, desire, and fear may arise, yet they do not touch the depth of presence that watches them.

This is liberation: flowing with life without being carried away, witnessing without clinging, and existing without separation.

Every illusion—of permanence, identity, or necessity—fades in this light. The mind may continue to weave its stories, but the awakened heart knows they are only passing forms. Life itself is a reflection, a play of appearances, yet the observer is eternal.

To be lost but alive is to realize that the freedom we seek was never outside. It was never something to acquire, to fight for, or to chase. It has always been within, in the silent, vast awareness that underlies all experiences. In this realization, there is no fear, no striving, no lack—only the eternal, unbroken presence of being.

Liberation in awareness is a quiet revolution. It does not shout or demand. It simply is, and in its presence, all things find their place, all illusions lose their grip, and the soul rests.

FREEDOM IS NOT OUTSIDE. IT IS THE AWARENESS THAT SEES THROUGH ALL ILLUSIONS. BE LOST BUT ALIVE, AND YOU ARE LIBERATED.

Epilogue

Time moves on, yet some feelings remain. One-sided love does not disappear; it does not vanish with words or tears. It becomes a quiet part of you, woven into the way you breathe, the way you pause, the way you remember. And perhaps that is its gift—its cruel, tender, enduring gift.

I have learned that survival is not about forgetting or moving on. It is about carrying the love that once consumed you with grace, letting it shape you without letting it break you. Each unanswered question, each unshared glance, each silent moment becomes a thread in the tapestry of who you are—a map of your resilience, your capacity to feel, and your quiet courage.

Even in its solitude, love teaches. It teaches patience, introspection, and the depth of the human heart. It teaches that beauty can exist in absence, that strength can live in sorrow, and that life can be profoundly meaningful even when it does not give you what you desire.

And so I walk forward, carrying the echo of a love that was never mine, yet became everything I needed to learn. I am still hollowed, still aching—but I am alive. I am present. I am whole in my solitude.

In the silence of unreturned love, I have found my voice. In the depth of unanswered questions, I have found myself. Lost, yet alive, I continue.